"Fast-paced, satisfying horror...a compelling read thanks to skillfully composed prose that builds tension and evokes emotional response."

—PUBLISHERS WEEKLY

"The tone and building dread reminds me of classic Stephen King. Great velocity and impact, and super creepy. Don't go in the basement!"

—STEWART O'NAN

"Brian James Freeman's evocative tale about the dark corners of an artist's imagination is elegant and haunting."

—DAVID MORRELL

"Spooky stuff!"

—RICHARD MATHESON

"*The Painted Darkness* is a dark, terrifying, and deeply moving gem of a novella. Brian James Freeman managed to both scare me and move me to tears."

—TESS GERRITSEN

"With Straubian lyricism, Brian James Freeman evokes not only the irrational terrors of childhood, but addresses the roots of creativity and the vital importance of art. A very impressive achievement."

—BENTLEY LITTLE

"*The Painted Darkness* delves into territory that fascinates so many of us—the fine lines between beauty and horror, faith and fear, art and the unconscious. Both a wonderful allegory and a gripping read, Brian James Freeman has written a taut, memorable tale."

—MICHAEL KORYTA

THE
PAINTED
DARKNESS

THE
PAINTED
DARKNESS

BRIAN JAMES FREEMAN

2012

Brian James Freeman
PO Box 623
Forest Hill, MD 21050

Trade Paperback
First Printing February 2012

ISBN-13: 978-1469975184
ISBN-10: 1469975181

For Kathryn...

With many thanks to my parents, the Hockers, Richard Chizmar, Mindy Jarusek, Andrea Wilson, Norman Prentiss, Douglas Clegg, Matt Schwartz, Stewart O'Nan, Peter Straub, William Peter Blatty, David Morrell, Bentley Little, Tess Gerritsen, Richard Matheson, Michael Koryta, Norman Partridge, Andrew Monge, Serenity Richards, Mark Sieber, Nanci Kalanta, Robert Mingee, Robert Brouhard, Jill Bauman, Russell Dickerson, Gail Cross, and Brian Keene.

ENTERTAINING ART:
AN INTRODUCTION

by Brian Keene

If you spend any amount of time perusing online discussion forums devoted to literature—especially forums for genre literature—you'll sooner or later come across the standard debate regarding art versus entertainment. Each side has its proponents...and its detractors, as well. The argument usually goes something like this: Good literature should be a work of art, just like a painting or a sculpture or a film or a song. It should strive to transcend human boundaries and give us a glimpse of some universal truth. Genre fiction and bestsellers, as typified by books like *Twilight*, *The Da Vinci Code*, and the works of such popular authors as Nora Roberts, Zane

Grey, Dean Koontz, and Stephen King, are not art. They are written for and marketed to the masses as entertainment, and therefore, they are not art.

Well, fuck that noise.

Stephen King's 'Salem's Lot is an entertaining read, but it subtlety goes beyond merely spinning us a good yarn, and provides a fascinating and illuminating examination of the Death of Small Town America and thus, the death of the American Dream. Or how about Neil Gaiman? The man wields words the way Monet wielded a paintbrush. Read *American Gods*, *The Graveyard Book*, or any issue of *Sandman* and you'll certainly come away entertained— but you'll also emerge challenged and enriched for the experience. That's because they are art. Entertaining art, but art nonetheless. Or how about J.R.R. Tolkien's *Lord of the Rings* or Larry McMurtry's *Lonesome Dove*? Are you going to tell me they don't deserve to hang in a museum of literature as the classics they are?

Sometimes you want entertainment and sometimes you want art. And sometimes you want both. Art and entertainment can be synonymous. Not everyone achieves this, of course. But those that do—you never forget them.

Which brings me to Brian James Freeman. I am an entertainer. Brian is an artist. I first met him nearly ten years ago, when he was a bright-eyed young man fresh out of high school and I was an already embittered thirty-something struggling to make a living as a writer. In the decade since then, I've gone on to write over fifteen books and a metric fuck-ton of short stories, comic books, and other assorted works of fiction. In that same ten year span, Brian has written one novel (the excellent *Black Fire*) and one novella (the superb *Blue November Storms*). He is not prolific. He is not quick. He takes his time, laboring over every word and nuance. He is not merely a craftsman, giving the people what they want. Brian James Freeman is an artisan. Yes, his stories are entertaining. Atmospheric, gripping—fiction that will give you immense enjoyment, but they transcend that, as well. You can spend a satisfying weekend with them. You can take them to the beach or out onto your patio deck and have a good time. But if you look beyond that, if you view them as works of art hanging in a museum, you'll see truths revealed— about the human condition and creativity and life and death and all the little things that we take for granted each day. They aren't always pretty truths.

They aren't always welcome truths. But they are truths nevertheless—some of the most important truths of all.

The printed page is Freeman's canvas, and he is painting darkness.

Lose yourself in it.

Brian Keene

The world is but a canvas to the imagination.

—HENRY DAVID THOREAU

A man paints with his brains and not with his hands.

—MICHELANGELO

There was something awesome in the thought of the solitary mortal standing by the open window and summoning in from the gloom outside the spirits of the nether world.

—SIR ARTHUR CONAN DOYLE

THE BIRTH OF THE ARTIST

(1)

J ust start at the beginning, Henry's father once told him, and the rest will take care of itself.

These words of wisdom came during the waning hours of a beautiful March day when Henry was five years old—a day that began with a gift from Mother Nature and ended with the little boy running home as fast as his legs would carry him, bounding through the snowdrifts and dodging the thorny branches lining the path through the woods.

Once inside the safety of his family's home at the end of Maple Lane, Henry fell to the hardwood floor in his bedroom, exhausted, his skin scratched, the wounds burning like they were on fire. His hands were bruised and bloody.

Henry crawled under his bed and closed his eyes and he prayed like he had never prayed before. Not the type of praying he did at bedtime every night as his mother watched, and not the generic prayers he said every week in church with the rest of the congregation. For the first time in his life, he was directing his message straight to God Himself, and Henry's request was simple: please send a mighty angel to undo what had been done.

An hour later, the room grew dark as the sun vanished behind the mountains to the west, but Henry hadn't moved an inch. Exhaustion and fear wouldn't allow him. He still wore his yellow rain slicker; his clothing was soaked in sweat; his face was damp with tears. The snow melting off his winter boots had trickled across the hardwood floor, forming a puddle of dirty water.

Finally, after what felt like an eternity, Henry heard the house's front door open and close. A few minutes passed, but he didn't dare move. He held his breath as he listened to the floorboards creaking through the house. The footsteps stopped outside his room and Henry almost couldn't bring himself to watch as the door swung open.

A pair of heavy work boots crossed the room, every step a dull thud, and Henry let out a small cry. The boots stopped. The man's pants were stained with grease and grime and bleach. He took a knee next to the puddle of melted snow and, after a brief moment, he reached under the bed with his weathered, callused hand.

Henry grabbed onto the giant hand and his father pulled him out in one quick, smooth motion. He hadn't turned the lights on yet, but there was a bright beam of moonlight creeping past the curtains, slicing the bedroom in half. Henry stared into his father's big eyes, which seemed to glow in the sparkling light. His father was a bear of a man, but he gently lifted Henry and sat him on the bed like someone moving the most delicate of antiques. Henry sobbed while his father rocked him in his enormous arms— and for a while, this did nothing to make the little boy feel better.

His father whispered: "It'll be okay, Henry. Just start at the beginning and the rest will take care of itself."

And Henry, still shaking, told his father what had pushed him to the brink of his sanity that beautiful March afternoon: a series of events so terrible he wouldn't allow himself to remember them once he grew up. He did his best to describe what had caused him to run as fast as he could through the woods and to hide under the bed, as if the bed might protect him from the horrors he had witnessed, as if the misery chasing after him wouldn't be able to find him in the dark. As if the monsters would leave him alone there.

"Son," his father said when Henry had finished, "the monsters don't live in the dark corners waiting to pounce on us. They live deep in our heart. But we can fight them. I promise you, we can fight them and we can win."

Henry listened to his father's words, which were soothing and comforting and wise. Then his father suggested he get a piece of paper and some crayons. His father said, "I know something that'll help you feel better."

Henry did as his father instructed, and before the night was over he would be repeating a mantra:

I paint against *the darkness.*

Those words made Henry feel strong in a way he couldn't describe. The words opened doors within his mind; they set him free and gave him courage to face the night.

But in the end, would that courage and his father's wisdom be enough to truly save Henry from the monsters he feared so much? Or had he just delayed the inevitable?

The answer to those questions wouldn't be determined for another twenty years.

THE PRESENT

(1)

The Blank Canvas in the Farmhouse Attic

*T*hese days Henry has no memory of the events
that led him to hide under his bed when
he was five years old—and because of that his
father's advice has a different meaning for him.

Whenever a blank canvas is staring at Henry,
he hears his father say, *just start at the beginning
and the rest will take care of itself,* and then the
path into his troubled imagination becomes clear
enough for him to paint his demons and worries
away. Normally this process is second nature to
Henry, like breathing, but today something is
wrong.

Henry's hand caresses the silver crucifix
dangling from his neck—a nervous habit he

developed as a child—and he repeats his father's words while the grandfather clock downstairs ticks off the hours, but the canvas remains blank.

Whenever Henry closes his eyes, all he can see is a stone wall blocking the path he must follow to the images. The wall in his mind is not giving an inch, no matter how hard he pushes.

The strength of the wall worries Henry as he stands barefoot in the attic of the old farmhouse on this blustery winter afternoon. Today's creative block is lasting longer than any he has ever experienced; the wall has never been so tall and thick before.

Occasionally Henry paces the room, but mostly he stands facing the canvas, prepared to paint when the inspiration comes. The floor is rough, but that's part of the process. He doesn't want to get too comfortable.

The attic is long and narrow with small windows at both ends, a low ceiling, and no lighting at all—and that's fine with Henry. He has never used anything other than natural light to see his work. He has even painted by the light of the moon when the lunar cycle allowed. And sometimes, when the images in his head just become too much for him to endure in the middle of the night, Henry will come here to paint in the dark.

When he's painting, Henry travels into an extraordinary world of his own creation and it doesn't matter how bright or dark or hot or cold the room is once he crosses the threshold from reality into his imagination. He is immune to the problems and concerns and realities of the outside world. Only the images that need to escape his mind—which are often a byproduct of his fears in the real world, although he's not always aware of their significance—matter after he has traversed the familiar path to the fantastic lands of his own creation.

But today Henry simply stands in the attic, waiting for inspiration to come. His wife, Sarah, and their three-year-old son, Dillon, aren't home, so the house is deathly silent, with the exception of the grandfather clock and the growing fury of the winter storm.

Occasionally, Henry will stare at the snow falling on the slate roof shingles beyond the attic window. Sleet taps on the glass. The branches hanging from the big tree in the front yard are catching ice, growing heavy and bending at their tips. The gravel driveway leading to the winding country road is gray-turning-white. The brown grass of the lawn is still showing, just a little, but not for long. The heavy, dark clouds above aren't moving fast; this storm will dump a lot of snow tonight.

The family's blue minivan, which would normally be parked in the garage under that big tree, is currently in Pittsburgh, along with Henry's wife and son. Dillon loves car rides, but the visit to Sarah's parents was not planned and Henry hasn't spoken to his wife since the van drove away the night before. He silently watched from the attic window as they left.

The fight with Sarah was sudden and unexpected, like most bad things in life. Henry had just emerged from the cellar where he was taking care of their ancient steam boiler's twice-a-day maintenance cycle when Sarah looked up from the onions she was chopping and said:

"Henry, you were up there in your cave when I left for work this morning and you'll still be there when I'm fast asleep in our bed. Do you realize that?"

Henry stopped. He was in a hurry to get to the attic to continue his work on his newest painting—yesterday there had been no creative block at all, only the thrill of creation—and the only reason he was even in the kitchen was to get to the cellar. His fear of what might happen if he forgot to maintain the boiler every twelve hours was stronger than his fear of leaving his artwork unfinished.

"I'm not working *that* much," he replied.

In the corner of the kitchen, Dillon stopped playing with his toys and watched his parents with wide eyes. Above him was one of the kitchen windows. A dead rose vine scratched across the glass in the wind. The roses were beautiful during the summer when they covered the east side of the house, crawling up a large trellis to the roof, but Henry found the sight of the lifeless vines during the winter to be disturbing.

"Oh, Henry, that's bullshit," Sarah snapped. "Where have you been going in that head of yours lately?"

Sarah had never cursed in front of Dillon, but Henry still didn't quite comprehend how upset his wife was. He just wanted to return to his painting, the one of the princess in the dungeon. The painting was calling him to the attic. The painting wasn't completed yet and he couldn't leave the work half-finished. That simply wasn't possible. Henry opened his mouth and said….

Now Henry shakes his head. He doesn't need to remember what he said; thinking about the conversation makes him uncomfortable. Last night was the first time he and Sarah had ever fought so seriously that she decided to pack up Dillon and visit her parents for a while.

This development worries Henry—and he knows that worries are one of the big reasons the stone wall is blocking his path into his imagination. Worries always cause him creative problems, but they can also unleash some of his most innovative efforts. They are, unfortunately, a double-edged sword.

Just start at the beginning, and the rest will take care of itself.

Henry barely hears the words as he stares at the blank canvas perched on the easel. He finds his attention drifting to the window and the huge tree pregnant with ice. There's a darkness spreading across the world.

The darkness growing inside the house might be worse, but Henry doesn't notice it yet. He's too distracted by his creative troubles. Yet the darkness is there, and it's even colder than the night wind, and it'll be calling for Henry very soon, much louder than any painting ever has.

THE BIRTH OF THE ARTIST

(2)

The small brick house on Maple Lane was the center of Henry's childhood universe. His mother worked odd jobs from home until he was old enough for school, but once Henry was able to climb the stairs of the beat-up yellow school bus every morning, she returned to work at the hectic emergency room in the hospital in Pittsburgh.

Henry's mother often arrived home late at night, sometimes not even until the next morning, so when the dilapidated bus dropped Henry off after school, he was met by Ms. Winslow, the elderly widow who lived next door. She would look after Henry until his father—one of the maintenance men for the Black Hills Community

School—was finished with his work, usually after six o'clock.

Henry spent some of each afternoon watching television with Ms. Winslow, but he always found his way to the backyard sooner or later. The yard was simple and square, surrounded by evergreen hedges and bordered by the woods between his home and the Slade River—and Henry was a young boy with a big imagination, so the enclosed area could represent a million things in a million places on any given day.

With a baseball and a glove, the hedges encircling the yard became fences and Henry was the center fielder for the Pittsburgh Pirates. They always won the World Series thanks to his homerun in the bottom of the ninth in Game Seven.

With his toy gun holstered in his pocket, he was a cop on patrol or a soldier in a war zone. Either way, he was heroic and often suffered several dramatic flesh wounds until the triumphant moment he conquered the bad guys and saved the day.

With a mini-football in his hand, he became the running back and quarterback and wide receiver for the Steelers, leading his team to yet another Super Bowl victory. There was very little defense in his imaginary games.

But sometimes the yard wasn't big enough for Henry's imagination, and on these days he would sneak off into the woods behind the house, usually when Ms. Winslow was supposed to be watching him. She tended to get caught-up in her soap operas—her "stories" was what she called them, which always made Henry laugh, although he wasn't sure why.

On the days he felt the urge to roam, Henry would flip a bucket on the concrete patio where his father's grill idly gave witness and he would peek through the kitchen window. This vantage point gave him a clear view of the living room without bringing attention to himself so he could make sure Ms. Winslow was really caught up in one of her shows or maybe even napping with her head slumped to the side.

If she was sleeping, he could always tell: when awake, she was very involved in what she was watching. Her curled, gray hair would bounce as her head shook; her wrinkled hands would point things out to the people on the other side of the screen; and sometimes she would even shout, her voice carrying throughout the house.

Once Henry was certain the coast was clear, he crept across the lawn, as if there might still be an authority figure waiting to ambush him, and then he pushed through the bushes that sometimes served as the outfield fence for his baseball games. Past the threshold there were deer trails leading deeper into the woods, through the heavy undergrowth and the towering trees. Out in the woods, his imagination could truly run wild.

But on the morning that would change his life forever, an hour before sunrise, Henry was wide awake and he wasn't thinking about the woods… although they would call to him soon enough. He was tucked under his warm blankets, feeling like a freshly toasted marshmallow, staring at the glowing green stars his father had stuck on the ceiling years ago—and he was trying his hardest to go back to sleep and pretend he didn't have to pee so badly his belly burned.

Eventually, though, Henry knew there was no way he was going to sleep. He crawled out from under the covers, shivered as his bare feet settled on the hardwood floor, and he scurried off to the bathroom. He was finished and debating whether to flush, which might wake his parents, or not to flush, which might get him scolded in the morning, when he realized there was frost on the window above the toilet. He closed the lid without flushing and climbed up for a better look. There were thick ice particles on the glass and snow was clinging to the trees in the backyard. The lawn was buried under a blanket of white powder.

"Mom! Dad! It snowed!" Henry cried, jumping off the toilet and running to the hallway. He pushed open his parents' bedroom door and scampered into their room, leaping onto the bed between them.

"What's wrong?" his father mumbled, rolling over, blinking his eyes open in the darkness. His mother covered her head with a pillow and muttered something.

"It snowed, Dad, it snowed!" Henry cried.

"Are you sure you didn't imagine the snow?" his father asked, checking the clock on the nightstand. It wasn't much past six.

"No, Dad, it's real this time, I swear!"

"Okay, okay, go get dressed and we'll check it out together," his father replied, rubbing his eyes.

Henry didn't wait a moment to run back to his room and start digging through the closet for his snow pants. He tossed everything else over his shoulder, creating a lopsided pile of discarded clothing and toys in the middle of the floor.

As far as Henry the Child was concerned, today was going to be the best day of his life. Maybe the best day ever.

THE PRESENT

(2)

The Monster and the Princess

*S*tart *at the beginning, and the rest will take care of itself.*

Henry understands these words are true—they've never led him astray—but right now all he can do is stare at the huge oak tree outside his window. The view reminds him of a tree he once discovered in the woods behind his childhood home. There was something unusual about that particular tree, but his memory is faded and he doesn't try to delve into the thoughts. Some topics, he suspects, are better left buried.

Henry loves the home he and Sarah bought last summer, using their life's savings as the down payment, but he now understands how truly isolated it is. The former farm borders a state park on three sides and there's forest for as far as the eye can see. Dozens of streams and ponds are within a mile of the main house, too. This is the perfect place to raise a little boy; that was Henry's first thought when he and Sarah visited with the real estate agent last summer. A little boy and maybe even a man with a lot of little boy left inside of him—a description Sarah has lovingly tossed at Henry from time to time when he's lost deep in thought.

Henry touches the silver crucifix hanging around his neck and he watches the tree twist in the wind. Under the window is the painting he worked on yesterday, but he has placed the finished canvas against the wall so the image faces away from him. There are a dozen paintings in a row like this one, turned so they can't be seen— and although Henry can't remember the subject matter of most of them, he doesn't need to see yesterday's artwork to remember it.

There is a lot of red and gray and black flowing across the front of the canvas. The scene is set in an ancient dungeon, and not the type you'd find in any fairy tale. The rough stone walls are damp with blood. The dirt floor is littered with the bloody remains of hundreds of dead rats.

In the middle of the canvas, he painted a princess wearing a tattered gown standing between a lumbering monster and a small child. She has put herself in the path of certain death and there's a fierce determination in her eyes. She holds a sword in her right hand.

The monster leans forward like some kind of insane hunchback, growling and snarling with slimy teeth. Hidden in the dark shadows are dozens of red glowing eyes. Henry cannot remember the actual act of painting the image—which isn't unusual, he rarely recalls how the paint made its way onto the canvas once all is said and done—but when he finished, he wondered where this idea came from and why he didn't choose a dark knight or some more traditional villain for the setting. Why does he always return to the monster?

Henry never understands exactly why his paintings are what they are, no matter how many times he tries to decipher what's happening inside his mind. He simply paints or draws what he sees in his head, and doing so keeps his dreams sane.

Once, a few years ago, he stopped creating any kind of artwork for a week, just to see what would happen. The result was clear and instantly noticeable: his dreams became warped and disturbing. His future wife, who was then simply his girlfriend, claimed his mind needed to release its creativity, one way or another. The theory was good enough for Henry and now not a day goes by that he doesn't draw something. The work is his own form of therapy.

Henry's eyes shift from the back of yesterday's finished painting to today's blank canvas. The canvas stares at him and the sensation is unsettling. The white space has never felt so huge—like the emptiness is trying to pull him into an inescapable void. The fear of having hit a permanent creative roadblock is stronger than ever.

"Just start at the beginning," Henry whispers as he closes his eyes. He takes a deep breath and adds, "I paint *against* the darkness."

Finally, after hours of self-imposed isolation, stars appear in the empty place behind Henry's eyelids—and then there's a burst of color in the distance. The stone wall in his mind starts to crumble—a few pieces near the edges at first and then larger sections in the middle—and finally

Henry pushes through his accumulated worries to the place where the images are trapped, just waiting to be released.

Without even opening his eyes, Henry begins to paint. One stroke at a time. One color at a time. One step at a time, like the journey of a thousand miles. His toes curl on the cold wooden floor and he rocks on the balls of his feet.

Henry easily slips into the in-between world where he lives when he's working, half-asleep and half-awake and not totally aware of anything beyond the canvas and the scenes unfurling in his head. He paints and he translates those visions the best he can, releasing the images through his nimble fingers.

It won't be until much later that he'll realize he's painting the princess in the dungeon again.

THE BIRTH OF THE ARTIST
(3)

*L*ess than ten minutes later, Henry and his father were in the front yard, throwing snowballs and shoveling the driveway as the sun rose above the distant mountains. The wind created drifts taller than Henry, but he carved a path through them the best he could. The sky was clearing and a beautiful blue morning grew from the horizon as the sun rose, sending bright rays through the ice hanging from the trees and the gutters.

Soon the neighbors were awake and tending to their driveways and sidewalks, shovels clanking against the asphalt and concrete. Everyone waved to everyone else, or you at least nodded, even to the neighbors you didn't really know or speak with often. Henry's father finished their sidewalk and continued on until Ms. Winslow's sidewalk was done, too. Then he returned to his own driveway where his son wasn't having much luck clearing the snow with his little plastic shovel.

A few minutes later, Henry's mother opened the front door and called for Henry to come inside and have some hot chocolate. He and his father were near the end of the driveway—his father using the big coal shovel *his* father had handed down to him while Henry worked with his plastic shovel. Henry looked up at his father, trying to hide the exhaustion and the cold creeping into his bones. His father saw the fatigue, of course.

"Go inside, Henry, and help your mother with the hot chocolate so she gets it just right. But don't forget to save some for me!"

Henry smiled, tossed his shovel into the snow, and ran to the front door, which his mother was holding open. She tussled his hair as he passed by and she called after him to stop and take off his yellow rain boots. He didn't have snow boots yet, but these kept his feet warm and dry, which seemed good enough for his mother—as long as he didn't track snow through the house.

Henry drank his hot chocolate and watched his morning cartoons while his mother finished washing the dishes from the previous night's dinner. Henry waited patiently for his father to come inside so they could plan their big snow day together, but when Henry's father finished the driveway, he hurried to take a shower and soon after he announced he had to leave for work.

"Why, Dad? It snowed!" Henry said, dumbfounded. He and his mother had checked the local newscast a couple of times to confirm the schools were closed and Henry didn't have to get ready for the day right away like he did on a normal morning.

"Well, the schools are closed for students, but I have a job to do, even if there aren't going to be any kids in the classrooms," his father explained, tussling Henry's hair like his mother had earlier.

Henry wasn't pleased at all, and his mother saw this, so she offered to play with him until she had to leave for work. Although Henry loved his mother with all his heart, the offer just wasn't the same—but being smart for his age, he said nothing as he watched his father carefully steer the station wagon down the slick driveway, waving one last time as he pulled away.

THE PRESENT
(3)
The Boiler Gulps

Two hours *after Henry breaks through the* mental wall, a noise from the cellar awakens him from his creative half-coma, and he mutters a curse when he realizes what the sound is: the *thump-thump-thump* of the boiler gulping for oil while trying to expel its belly of built-up pressure.

The boiler can devour as much oil as it wants—and the big beast does, according to the hefty bill left on the front door every time Greensburg Oil & Gas fills the tank—but the unit cannot drain itself of the used water, and without proper drainage, the dirty water and the steam pressure can build and build until it has nowhere to go but through the weakest seams in the pipes.

The results could be deadly, a fact that isn't lost on Henry even when his mind is cluttered with other worries.

Henry forgot his morning maintenance session in the cellar today, and now the boiler is calling for him. Warning him in the only way it can.

Better get moving, boy, 'cause things are getting a bit tight in here.

Henry heeds the call and rushes down the attic stairs, past the family photos and the spacious rooms their unassuming furniture can't fill. He doesn't bother to stop and put on his shoes, although he should, considering what's waiting for him in the cellar.

Henry hurries into the brightly painted country kitchen where he and Sarah had their fight the night before. The cellar door is tucked to the left of the pantry almost as an afterthought. He grabs the glass doorknob in one smooth motion, picking up the heavy-duty flashlight off the kitchen counter at the same time.

Thump-thump-thump, calls the boiler.

"I hear you, you stupid fat bear," Henry replies, using his father's phrase without even realizing what he's saying.

He opens the door and flips the light switch. It flickers to life in a yellow burst above his head, but there's darkness beyond the bottom of the stairs. There are no additional lights down there, yet he catches a glimpse of a rat scurrying off into a corner. He shudders at the thought.

This is why his flashlight never travels far from the kitchen counter. There are no windows in the cellar. Only darkness and dampness and an uneven dirt floor—and the rats and centipedes and other bugs that mostly stay in the dark where they belong. Henry's attempts to exterminate them—traps and poisons—have failed, but at least he hasn't seen the little monsters anywhere other than in the cellar.

Henry stands on the top step, staring into the gloom, watching for anything else to pass through the slot of light at the bottom of the stairs.

Thump-thump-thump, calls the boiler.

Henry hears the sound, but the noise is suddenly miles away. His vision spins; the stairs twist and roll; the dim light flickers and flashes. The chipped stone walls sweat condensation and he hears the crackle of running water off in the distance. The sound is not really there. It's more like a memory he can't quite recall. But everything else is as real as his trembling hand pressed to the damp wall. He shivers.

Thump-thump-thump.

Henry stands at the top of the stairs, one hand clutching the slim metal railing, and he closes his eyes. The vast darkness behind his eyelids spins; he sees colors in the darkness, the same kind of colors that come to him when he's painting. Bright white stars burst to life in the distance. His fingers tighten on the railing, but he doesn't step backwards, he doesn't sit. He remains standing.

Henry isn't afraid of the dark; he knows the dark intimately. In fact, he has learned to embrace the darkness and control his terrors to his own benefit. His paintings appeal to collectors who still worry about monsters lurking in the darkest corners of their bedrooms and deep in their hearts.

Once, when asked why his work features terrible events happening to perfectly good people, Henry had simply replied: *I paint* against *the darkness.*

He never quite understood why those words were so important, but now, as he stands at the top of the spinning stairs, the phrase floats inside his eyelids, the bright red letters hovering in the star-spotted blackness. The stars spin clockwise and the words twist and rotate counterclockwise.

"I paint *against* the darkness," Henry whispers, his voice foreign to his own ears.

When he opens his eyes, the rickety wooden stairs have returned to normal. They are steep and narrow but passable. They do not twist or roll. The walls are merely damp. There is no running water anywhere. The light above his head is steady and dim. It isn't a beautiful light, but rarely has Henry considered any light to be beautiful. Light is, after all, only the absence of darkness.

Thump-thump-thump.

"Get a grip, Henry," he whispers. "*This* is the kind of foolish crap Sarah was talking about."

Henry descends the stairs, his flashlight burning a path through the dark. He keeps a hand on the railing and he remains steady. At the bottom of the steps, he surveys the cellar, shining the flashlight from side to side.

Rats with beady eyes scamper further into the darkness, fleeing the light. They dart behind the tables and empty cabinets of the old workshop the previous owner left behind and which Henry can't imagine ever using. They sprint into the maze of rusted old rakes, shovels, and hoes. The former owner had been in the process of repairing the tools to sell at the local flea market when he broke his hip and was forced to leave his lifelong home for good. The stairs were too much for him to handle at his advanced age.

Henry doesn't know for certain whether or not the rats were here when the former owner worked in the cellar, but now they squeeze into the tiny cracks and holes in the stone walls as if there's a network of tunnels through the foundation where the rats live and sleep and fornicate. That thought also makes Henry shudder.

The cellar ceiling is low and constructed of crisscrossing timbers. Henry must stoop to avoid hitting his head, even though he has never been mistaken for a tall man at any point in his life. The floor is hard dirt, packed solid and tight but uneven. The walls remind Henry of a photograph he once saw in a news magazine: the tiny, hidden cell where a prisoner of war had been tortured to death. Those walls were also wet.

It's no wonder the real estate agent tried to avoid showing Henry and Sarah this cellar when they first toured the property. But when the agent mentioned the steam-powered heating system, Henry had insisted on seeing the boiler for himself. His father had worked with steam boilers and Henry wasn't sure about having one in his own home as an adult. They were loud, often clanging like a demon was loose in the pipes, and the older models weren't exactly renowned for their ease of use.

More importantly, they could be dangerous. If you weren't careful, you could be injured, maimed, or even killed.

Thump-thump-thump.

The boiler calls for Henry again and he points his flashlight to where the beast hulks, huge and ugly. The center section is round and as black as a moonless night. There are a dozen pipes snaking in every direction from the main body, curving and twisting like a roller coaster with no end. Next to the unit is the enormous oil tank, which has been refilled three times already this winter.

The boiler gulps the oil, Henry once told his wife, and she gave him a funny look.

It gulps, you know? he said earnestly. She smiled and laughed and touched his face with the gentle understanding of a mother whose child isn't making much sense. She didn't understand, but he did, and that was what mattered.

Henry stares at those pipes; he studies them closely. Sometimes in his dreams the pipes come to life, quietly shaking loose, stretching and reaching like arms with giant hands. In these same dreams, the faceplate on the boiler inevitably blows open, sending a wave of flames rolling across the dirt floor to engulf him, and the boiler growls and says: *You were right, Henry, I gulp and I gulp until there's nothing left!*

Henry always wakes with a start from these dreams, although he knows they aren't real. There *are* monsters in the world, but they're not the bogeymen of children's stories. Still, after the nightmares, he often slips out of bed and sneaks to his attic studio to paint the darkness away. He paints until his mind and his heart are calm. Then he returns to bed and sleeps like a baby.

The pipes and the main body of the boiler are wrapped in asbestos, which has been encapsulated by thick coats of paint over the years. But the paint is old and flaking, and many of the sections have crumbled into chalky piles on the dirt floor.

"Ah hell, asbestos gets a bad rap," Henry says, quoting his father. "If you don't burn it and breathe in the flames, and if you don't sniff big piles of the dust, you're good to go. It's the best insulation there is."

Henry doesn't understand why he's standing motionless at the bottom of the steps instead of getting the job done so he can return to his work in the attic, but he senses there's something wrong. He can't put his finger on what the problem is, and nothing appears to be out of place, but Henry's father taught him to trust his gut and never take chances when it comes to a big old steam boiler, which is essentially a pressure bomb ticking away in the basement of your home. A profound coldness has wrapped around Henry, chilling his arms and legs and closing in on his heart. He shivers; something is truly wrong and he has no idea what it could be.

Thump-thump-thump.

The boiler continues to call, but Henry stands silently in the darkness, unable to move, his legs frozen by a strange fear he can't explain.

Thump-thump-thump.

THE BIRTH OF THE ARTIST

(4)

*A*fter Henry's father left for work, Henry knew he should still be thrilled: *he* didn't have to go to school today, after all. Now he needed to decide what to do, and the answer to that question was easy, too. There was a big back yard full of snow waiting for him. What *couldn't* he do?

As Henry dressed himself in his snow pants and the yellow rain boots, his mind filled with possibilities. *No school!* He actually liked going to school and seeing his friends and his teacher, but the idea of being home on a day he was supposed to be in the classroom was exhilarating, like getting away with breaking a stupid rule.

A few moments later Henry's mother came into his room, where he was sitting on the floor trying to buckle the latches on his boots. She was dressed for her job as a triage nurse in the hospital's emergency room, which the snowstorm had left more short-staffed than normal.

"Going to play in the snow?" she asked.

"Yep!"

"Have fun and be safe. I have to go to work, but Ms. Winslow will watch you."

"No snow day for you *and* Dad?" he asked.

"Sorry, love, but duty calls." She kneeled and helped Henry with his boots. Then she smoothed the part in his hair with her fingers. Her nails were freshly painted. "You be good for Ms. Winslow. Be my Big Boy, okay?"

"I will."

"And promise me you'll stay away from the woods."

"I promise," he lied without missing a beat.

In the summer, the growth of the woods beyond the yard was thick and wild, but if he made it through the bushes and prickers and weeds safely, there was a well-worn path along the Slade River where he could skip stones on the water or catch a frog with his bare hands. Today the river would be icy and there would be no frogs, but he wasn't the least bit interested in the frigid water. He had another destination in mind.

Back in the heaviest growth, just short of the river, was where Henry had discovered the old abandoned pick-up truck the previous summer. The tires and seats were rotted, the paint was nearly gone, the frame was rusted, and it was sitting a mile from the nearest road with no easy way to explain how any kind of motor vehicle could have gotten there. Henry's best guess involved something he had seen while watching the New Year's Day *Twilight Zone* marathon with his father.

The truck wasn't the only hidden treasure to be discovered in those woods—and *that* was what really excited Henry's imagination. The best thing he ever found—besides the truck and the dozens of antique Coke bottles and a broken fishing rod and even the rusted barrel of a flint rifle— was a forgotten tree house, nestled high in the limbs of a soaring oak with a thousand branches. The majestic tree stood alone in the middle of a clearing, rising above the rest of the forest like a mighty tower.

There wasn't a rope ladder to the tree house any more, but sometimes Henry thought if he were just a little bit taller he might be able to reach the lowest branch and climb the rest of the way. He daydreamed about what he might find up there, and he fought the urge to tell anyone else about it, even his father. The clearing and the giant oak were meant to be a secret place. Somehow he knew that deep down where he kept all of his secrets.

Henry loved his adventures in the woods, but he had to be careful, too. He had a bad scare the first time he wandered off the trail—a mistake he knew to never make again—and the older kids at school had already filled his head with stories of monsters from beyond the grave who supposedly haunted the forest. Henry knew enough not to believe the stories, yet deep down, he thought *maybe* they could be true, at least a little. For a little boy with a big imagination, that was enough.

The warnings didn't stop Henry from wandering off the trail occasionally, of course. He was careful in the woods—people sometimes really did go missing along the river—but there was so much cool stuff to be found away from the trails and he wanted to explore the land until he knew all of its secrets.

And today the woods presented a whole new world, one covered under a thick blanket of snow and ice. So even as Henry had been dressing himself to play in the backyard, he knew where he was really headed on this perfect snow day.

His day would be spent exploring the woods.

And that was how he would discover the monsters in the real world.

THE PRESENT

(4)

The Darkness Below the House

The boiler needs to be drained and refilled every twelve hours during the winter, and the previous owner left Henry a helpful note explaining all five steps of the process very clearly. Henry had discovered the handwritten instructions tacked to the cellar door the day his family moved into their new home. He knew all about steam boilers from his father, of course, but he appreciated the kindness of the previous owner, the man who had lived here all his life, leaving behind the workshop and those rusty tools in the cellar as his legacy.

A modern unit can do the five maintenance steps automatically, but the boiler in this cellar is anything but modern. Actually, Henry is pretty sure it was original with the house. Somewhere along the way someone upgraded the unit to oil from coal, but the idea of adding any kind of new and automated controls is laughable. Henry hopes to replace the boiler once and for all in the spring if their finances allow. The new unit will handle the five twice-a-day maintenance steps automatically, controlled by a thermostat on the first floor. Henry will never have to visit the cellar again if all goes well.

Right now, though, Henry stands frozen in place, unable to perform the tasks he came here to do. Something feels very wrong in the cellar. Maybe it's those damn rats or maybe the sensation is an aftereffect of the vertigo, but his arms are covered in goosebumps and his heart is racing. He senses movement in the periphery of his vision, but when he swings the flashlight around, there's nothing to be seen. Then:

Thump-thump-thump, the boiler calls.

The hulking mass emits a burp from deep inside the heavy cast iron belly—and Henry laughs, the tension broken by the sound.

"What the hell are you doing?" he asks himself, shaking his head in disbelief. "It's just a boiler! And I know how to handle a fat bear."

Henry laughs again and crosses the cellar, the dirt cold on his feet as he hunches over to avoid hitting his head on the wooden beams. Bending like this at his hips comes naturally enough after a few months of navigating the space twice a day. The flashlight guides him past the rough spots in the dirt-packed floor. Henry wishes he had put his shoes on, but now he just wants to finish the work and get upstairs where his paints and canvas are waiting for him.

Thump-thump-thump.

The first step of the maintenance routine is simple enough. Henry flips the metal toggle switch on the side of the unit from ON to OFF. As the previous owner had written in his note, *This baby's a gulper and you don't want her gulping while you have her valves open!*

After that's done, Henry moves to the second step. On the other side of the boiler is a spigot with a rusted cut-off valve. Below the spigot is a metal bucket with a broken wooden handle. Henry keeps meaning to replace the bucket, but somehow he never gets around to it. Too many other things to fix in the house, he reasons, although he isn't entirely satisfied with his explanation.

After double-checking to confirm the bucket is in place, Henry cranks the rusted valve. The valve creaks, the pipes shake, and then there's a thunderous belch of steam as the boiling black water spits into the bucket, which screams from the sudden heat. The boiler groans in pain, too. The water is as dark as the thick oil the boiler gulps.

Henry's father had given this process a lot of nicknames, but "draining the fat bear" is probably the one Henry remembers the best. He always thinks of his old man while performing this five-step act of home maintenance each day. His father spoke fondly of the steam boilers he cared for at work. They even had names. Always girls' names. Hillary, Matilda, Gertrude, Amelia. That's probably why his father saying his most important duty was to "drain the fat bears" always made Henry laugh as a child.

After fifteen seconds, the water spitting from the spigot is relatively clear and the bucket is full of the thick black goop. Henry twists the valve back in the opposite direction until the steam and water stop; the pipe bucks and groans. He then lets the bucket sit for a few moments so the metal can cool.

While he waits, Henry considers the potential danger if he ever fails to heed the boiler's warnings and needs. Eventually the system would overheat and burn the whole house down—or, if things went really wrong, the boiler could explode. There were no safety shutoffs on models manufactured when people were still dependent on horses to make the trek to town, after all. No gauges or emergency breakers, either. You have the unit OFF or you have it ON, and if it's ON, you'd better be paying attention because it can get mighty hot and mighty pissed off, as Henry's father would say.

The third step is a lot like the second step, only sort of in reverse. Henry reaches up to the top of the boiler's main body where a pipe from the outside wall runs into the unit. There's another rusting shutoff valve there and he cranks it clockwise from the CLOSED position to OPEN— or at least as open as the calcium-filled pipes get these days. There's a cold hissing sound as clean, clear mountain water rushes into the boiler's system. Henry can't see the water, of course, but he can imagine it. Imagining things has never been a problem for him. Quite the opposite, as Sarah reminded him last night.

After fifteen seconds—he counts in his head, no need for him to look at his watch with the flashlight—he twists the valve to the CLOSED position. Now that the system has fresh water, it'll be good to go for another twelve hours.

Just two more steps and Henry's work will be completed.

Next he places his flashlight on the dirt floor and he picks up the bucket. He shuffles his way toward step number four, which is to carefully tip the contents of the bucket into the circular metal grating covering the drain in the middle of the dirt floor. The drain is merely a pipe leading into a pit under the house dug by the original builders. A reasonable amount of liquid can be poured into the pit, but if you put in too much, it'll simply back up into the cellar. And, as the former owner cheerfully explained in his handwritten instructions, *Don't piss in the drain unless you want the funk to linger for weeks.*

Henry carries the steaming bucket of black sludge water with both hands, one on each side of the broken wooden handle. Steam rises, condensing on his flesh. He follows the beam of light from his flashlight and he carefully sets the bucket next to the rusted metal drain.

Henry wipes his hands on his shirt, and after another moment of rest, he tips the bucket forward as gently as he can considering he's using the broken handle for leverage.

That's when Henry sees the big red eye blinking up at him from the bottom of the drain, and that's when he hears the growl of the beast for the first time.

That's also the last thing Henry remembers until he awakens on his kitchen floor hours later, ice cold and bleeding from the forehead with burns on his scalded right hand.

THE BIRTH OF THE ARTIST
(5)

Ms. *Winslow was deeply immersed in a game* show less than ten minutes after she arrived to watch Henry, but those were the longest ten minutes of his life. He tried to concentrate on other things to pass the time, but all he really wanted to do was sneak into the woods and explore the icy landscape. To anyone observing him, he might have looked just a tad bit crazy as he quickly paced around the backyard, his bright yellow rain slicker and boots reflecting the morning sunlight all around him as he moved.

Finally, on the tenth time Henry stood on the overturned bucket on the snowy concrete slab and looked through the kitchen window, he saw exactly what he was waiting for: Ms. Winslow shaking her hand at the television screen, doing her best to urge a contestant on the game show toward the correct answer.

Henry jumped off the bucket and ran across the yard. He shoved through the barren bushes under the big tree at the edge of their property and a wave of ice and snow rained down on him. He didn't care if he got wet. The sight beyond his yard took his breath away. The woods were even more beautiful than he expected: everything white and pristine. He realized no one, not even an animal, had been through the area since the snow stopped. He felt like he was the first human explorer to find an undiscovered land.

Henry gazed up at the icicles hanging from the tree branches; they glowed bright white in the cool winter sunlight. The whole world was like that: radiant and vibrant and picturesque.

Soon, though, the peace was broken as Henry went bounding along the deer trails, his index finger extended to form the shape of a gun. He was a top-secret soldier on a top-secret mission behind enemy lines in a top-secret war. His cover had been blown, and he was on the run, firing over his shoulder, picking off his pursuers with frightening accuracy. Bullets whizzed past him and he ducked and rolled through the snow, firing and hitting one bad guy and then another and another. When he spotted an elite enemy sniper perched in a tree, Henry dove and fired from the hip. The bad guy screamed, spun, and fell through the branches, sending a cascade of ice and snow crashing to the ground with a roar like thunder.

When Henry played the Top Secret Soldier game or his Cops and Robbers game or any of the Win The Big Game games, he could see everything as clearly as if the people were really real: the soldiers, the spies; the cops, the robbers; his teammates and even the crazed fans in the stands.

Henry had sort of assumed everyone else could conjure up playmates, too, but he was starting to have his doubts. The kids at school played the normal games together during recess, while he sat alone and imagined crazy new games he could play all by himself in his head. His adventures were as real as any story his father read to him at bedtime or anything Henry saw on television, but recently he told his father this and his old man laughed and said:

My boy, you're never going to run out of imagination.

Henry didn't know what that meant, and from the way his mother looked at him after he talked about his imaginary worlds, he had the feeling he shouldn't tell anyone else. Doing so might not be such a hot idea. If he was the only one who could make up things and have them seem so real, telling people was probably just asking for trouble. He saw how the kids at school who were "different" were treated, and he was happy to just be left alone when he consider the alternative.

Henry was still sprinting through the woods, pushing branches to the side, and it wasn't too long before he burst through another thick grove of icy bushes, sending frozen chunks of snow flying everywhere. He stopped dead in his tracks, stunned by the beautiful sight he had stumbled upon: the hidden clearing in the thickest part of the woods.

Henry had been here before, but he was surprised to see the snow had been blown against the big oak tree, the one with the dilapidated tree house. In fact, the snow had piled up in such a way that Henry was certain he could reach the lowest branch—which meant he could finally discover what was hidden in the dark confines of the tree house placed firmly in the high branches.

THE PRESENT

(5)

Burns and Bumps and Bruises

When *Henry awakens on the kitchen floor,* the linoleum is ice-cold under his body. Before he understands how badly his right hand is burned, before he can comprehend what the stickiness under his left hand must be, he knows he never completed step number five in the twice-a-day boiler maintenance program. He didn't turn the unit back on. It sits down there, hungry and empty, and the house has sucked in the chill of the winter storm blowing through the valley. His skin is like ice.

Then the pain in his right hand comes roaring into his brain and Henry screams. In this moment he doesn't care about the temperature; he envies the cold. He wants the cold to wrap around his skin again and extinguish the fire raging in his fingers.

Henry rolls onto his side, through the congealing blood from the wound on his forehead, and he pushes himself to his knees. He gets to his feet and flips the light switch. His hand is badly burned: red and purple and nearly black in places, the skin loose and flabby. Another scream rises in his throat.

Be calm, his father's voice whispers in Henry's mind. Maybe this should alarm Henry, but it isn't the first time he's heard his father since the old man died. He often remembers his father's words of wisdom in his father's own voice and he finds this to be soothing. *Be calm and take things one step at a time.*

Henry does not scream again. The voice is right. He knows how to treat burns; he can handle this. He breathes in deeply and thinks through the process.

The first step is to soak the affected area. He stumbles to the sink, knocks the stopper in place with his good hand, and starts a stream of cool water. This will hurt at first, but then it will help. He gently lowers his aching hand as the water rises. He grits his teeth and looks away. The window above the sink is covered with frost and the big snowflakes are still falling.

"It's dark," Henry says, reaffirming how much time has passed since…since when? He has no idea how he came to be in this state. He recalls working on a painting and then running downstairs to feed the boiler and then…what?

Henry reaches for the cabinet next to the window and retrieves the bottle of extra strength aspirin. He pops the bottle open with his thumb and swallows four of the white pills without a drink.

After a few minutes, he lifts his hand from the water and gently pats the wound dry. Next he applies his wife's aloe vera cream from the same cabinet where he got the aspirin. The affected area aches, but the immediate burning sensation and the howling pain have dimmed.

After he wraps a gauze bandage around his hand again and again, Henry surveys the room. There is a puddle of blood on the floor where he had been laying. He touches his forehead, feels the stickiness on his scalp.

"I'm a mess," he says. "What the hell did I do?"

He still can't remember what happened, but he cleans the small gash on his forehead, washing the wound and patting it dry with a clean paper towel. The bleeding has stopped, but he applies a large bandage to be safe. He probably needs to visit the emergency room, but that's a good thirty minute drive in the best of weather, and this is not the best of weather.

The back door's window is coated with ice and frost. Henry unlocks the deadbolt and opens the door, but a gust of frigid winter wind knocks him backwards. Snow is blowing hard across the glacial winter landscape; the sight is beautiful in a ferocious kind of way. There's at least two feet of snow with several inches of ice mixed in for good measure.

Henry isn't driving anywhere. Even if he did venture across the lawn to the snow-packed garage under the big tree, his little Honda isn't up to the challenge. He wouldn't get out of the garage, let alone through the snow dunes between him and the two-lane road that won't be plowed until morning.

Henry closes the door, locks it. The winter wind gusts against the house and the coldness pushes deeper into his core. The aching in his bones isn't just from his wounds. The winter chill is inside the house, gnawing into him.

The cold jogs his memory. The *thumping* of the boiler. The twice-a-day maintenance. The red eye blinking at him from the darkness of the drain.

Henry does the only thing a grown man can do upon remembering such a series of events: he laughs.

"An eye in the drain?" he says. As bad as the wounds on his body are, he can't believe what he thought he saw. He laughs again. What else can he do?

Henry is about to head downstairs to take care of maintenance step number five—turning the boiler on so it can gulp the oil and send steam throughout the house into the metal radiators— when the phone rings. The sound startles him. He hadn't realized how bad his hands were shaking until this moment; his entire body is rocking.

Henry hurries to the phone and answers, but there's only silence on the line.

"Hello?" he says. "Sarah?"

There's a brief burst of static, the crackle of a voice, and the line goes dead. Henry hangs up and tries to dial the number for the condo in the city, but there's no dial tone. He's not terribly surprised. He lives in the middle of nowhere and phone problems aren't uncommon, even in this fiber optic day and age. He waits in the kitchen for a few more minutes, hoping he might get lucky and the phone will ring again, but there's nothing.

Henry returns to the top of the cellar stairs. His trusty flashlight, which sits next to the boiler where he left it, is cutting a bright corridor through the darkness.

Thump-thump-thump.

Henry cocks his head, puzzled. This sound isn't from the boiler. The boiler is switched off, after all. The boiler is metallic and big. This noise was small and wet.

Henry stands motionless while his frazzled brain attempts to decipher what he could have heard.

Thump-thump-thump.

And this time, the flashlight moves.

And then comes a growl, deep and guttural, like the one that greeted him when he looked into the cellar drain.

Henry's instincts take control and he's bolting through the living room and up the stairs before the flashlight in the cellar has even settled back into place.

THE BIRTH OF THE ARTIST

(6)

Henry stared at the tree house, which seemed larger and more dangerous than he remembered—maybe because he could finally climb up there and discover what was hidden inside. The snowdrifts had blown around the base of the mammoth tree, forming something like a ramp to the lowest branch. From there it would just be a matter of careful climbing. He had climbed smaller trees; he knew he could do it.

So why was there such a tight knot swelling in his stomach?

Henry reached for the lowest branch. That was his only answer to the questions his body was asking him. He climbed and he kept his eyes locked on the next branch. All he could do was keep moving. He imagined what he must look like to someone watching him: the bright yellow rain slicker slowly ascending the thick trunk of the tree.

A few minutes later, the winter air was biting at Henry's fingers through his gloves; his hands and his feet were starting to ache. To make matters worse, the wind was gusting, blowing chunks of ice and snow off the branches, pummeling him as he climbed. Twice he almost lost his grip, and his stomach lurched into his throat each time.

When he finally arrived at the bottom of the tree house, Henry gasped in relief. He reached for the latch that held a trap door in place. He struggled to release the metal latch, which seemed to be frozen in place. He debated taking off his right glove to get a better grip, but he quickly dismissed the idea. His hands were cold enough.

Henry stood on his tippy toes to gain more leverage; his legs were wobbly. He grunted and put all of his weight into turning the latch—which suddenly gave way, flipping to the side. The heavy wooden door swung open faster than Henry had expected, passing within inches of his face. He was so startled he almost stepped backwards. His eyes instinctively shifted to the ground far below the barren tree branches covered in ice and snow.

Henry stared in horror as the ground zoomed up at him and his world began to spin. He felt himself falling...but he wasn't moving. His insides were merely anticipating the descent he sensed was coming; his mind was readying for the shock of hitting those branches on the way down, followed by the frozen slap of the snow-covered ground.

The world continued to spin and Henry couldn't stop staring; he was mesmerized by the ground that seemed to be lunging up at him. His center of gravity shifted as the winter wind whipped past his face.

The icy air on his cheeks shook Henry from his daze. He wrapped his arms around the tree trunk and he turned his head. He would fall if he didn't move. He reached through the trap door, grabbed on to the edge, and started to pull himself to safety. For a moment he thought he wouldn't have the strength to make it, but then he braced his yellow rain boot against a branch and launched himself through the opening like a champagne cork being popped.

Henry rolled across the floor, closed his eyes, and breathed in deeply while pulling his knees to his chest, rocking himself gently. He knew this wasn't the Big Boy way to handle the situation, but he couldn't help himself. He was more scared by the near disaster than he had ever been in his entire life.

He could still feel himself almost falling, and he understood for the first time how easily death could come for anyone, even little boys. He wasn't sure if he believed in the Heaven and the Hell the preacher at church talked about, and he definitely wasn't sure where little boys who snuck off into the woods were sent when it came to the afterlife, but he was certain he would rather not learn the answers to those questions anytime soon.

Once his breathing had returned to normal, Henry opened his eyes. The roof of the old structure was partially collapsed and the dark wood of the walls and floor were rotten in places. There were crude windows on three sides and Henry could see he was above the rest of the trees. The gray clouds swirled through the valley, the wispy remains of the unexpected winter storm.

Henry turned to look for the trap door—he didn't want to fall through when he moved—and that was when he saw the skeleton sitting in the far corner.

And that was when Henry screamed.

The wordless sounds coming from his throat didn't even sound human to him, much less like any noise he could willfully make—and for a moment he was certain the shriek had come from the skeleton. His scream echoed through the woods.

After a moment, though, Henry stopped. He tried to calm himself the way his mother would if she were here. He had already acted like a baby once today; he was supposed to be a Big Boy. Yes, the skeleton was scary, but it couldn't hurt him, right? A skeleton was a person who had been dead for a long time, and a dead person was a sad thing, but the dead couldn't hurt the living. His parents had explained this to him once while dressing him in his Sunday church outfit on a Tuesday morning, the day of his grandmother's funeral the previous summer.

Now Henry studied the skeleton of a child about his age. The skull was grinning. The skeleton wasn't as scary as Henry first thought, but what did frighten him was the tattered yellow rain slicker and the boots—they reminded him of what he was wearing.

Henry closed his eyes and took a series of deep breaths. When he opened his eyes again, the skeleton was gone.

The bones hadn't even existed in the first place, and Henry had no idea what to think now. It was as if one of the games he liked to play in the yard had gotten out of hand—as if the line between his imagination and the real world had blurred and he didn't even realize it *was* a game.

Henry stood and approached the corner where the bones had been, careful to avoid the trap door.

There were no bones, but there was a necklace. The silver was tarnished. Henry picked up the chain, tentatively touched the metal Christ hanging from the loop. The metal was cold and he wondered where the necklace had come from. Why would someone leave something like this in a tree house? How could it have been forgotten? What happened to the previous owner?

Henry dropped the necklace in his pocket, put his hands on the crude window, and gazed out over the endless forest and the snow-covered river in the distance. The sight was beautiful, but Henry was concerned by the coldness he felt tightening inside himself, as if he was still on the verge of falling. Only the height wasn't what made him nervous. His parents always said he was a thoughtful boy and he accepted he spent more time just thinking about stuff than other kids, but he didn't know how to be any other way. He simply was the way he was.

So Henry stood in the empty tree house and he stared at the snowy winter landscape and he contemplated what was happening in his ever-expanding world of youthful magic and wonder.

A few moments later, right as he felt the floor crumbling under his feet, he noticed the movement in the bushes beyond the clearing: thousands of white rabbits with dark red eyes, all of them bounding through the woods like a herd of cattle.

But before Henry could really grasp the bizarreness of the spectacle, his entire world flipped upside down and he was falling for real.

THE PRESENT
(6)
A Brave Man or a Coward

Henry the Adult has never considered himself to be either a brave man or a coward, but now he knows which side of the fence he falls on when strange things happen. He's a coward and he plans on having no problem telling everyone that once he learns what made the sound in the cellar. And what moved the flashlight.

Henry sits in the attic and listens to the storm blowing against his house. He's a grown man and there must be a reasonable explanation for what happened. He tells himself this because he understands it's what he's supposed to believe as an adult.

The problem is, Henry thinks as he sits in the darkened attic with the door locked, *there is* not *a good explanation.*

Sometimes he may spend hours lost in his imagination, certain there are mysterious forces at work in the universe that allow him to take the worries in his head and transform them into beautiful and disturbing images painted on a canvas, but he's not ready to admit there could actually be some kind of monster in his cellar. Those kinds of thoughts open the doors to madness. There must be a better explanation.

"Those stupid rats!" Henry cries, quickly latching on to the sanest idea his semi-hysterical mind can conjure. "Could they have made that sound? They certainly could have moved the flashlight, right? Of course they could! They're always moving crap down there."

Which was true. Sometimes, when he and Sarah were in the kitchen, they'd hear the clang of the rusty tools being knocked together. Sometimes it even sounded like the cabinet doors in the old workshop were opening and closing as the rats searched for food and supplies to build their nests in the foundation walls and wherever else they might roam.

Henry isn't convinced the rats were the source of the sound and the movement, but he is an adult—a grown man with a wife and a child—and he understands he's not allowed to accept the possibility there might really be monsters in the world. Not until he exhausts every natural explanation, no matter how strange.

Henry unlocks the attic door and heads downstairs.

THE BIRTH OF THE ARTIST
(7)

One moment Henry was gazing through the crudely made window at the snow-covered forest, the next moment everything had gone black. He had no idea where he was and he couldn't remember what had happened, but when he blinked open his eyes the world was very dark and very wet—and an extremely heavy weight was pressing on his chest.

Then images and sounds flashed into his mind:

The creaking of the tree house crumbling under his weight.

His terrified attempt to grab on to the window.

The plummet through the branches, which smacked at him like the heavy fists of the biggest bully at school.

Then his memories collided with a wall of darkness.

Henry rolled over, blinking until the blurry winter light stopped spinning. He was deep in the snow bank at the base of the tree. He stared into the gray and blue sky, bewildered, watching the clouds gliding to the east.

Henry had lost his gloves somewhere along the way, and his entire body ached, and his heart was racing, and he was breathing hard—and best of all, he was alive!

Henry spotted the jagged hole in the floor of the tree house high above. He thought about the skeleton he had imagined for a moment, the one wearing a yellow rain slicker and boots. He slipped his hand into his pocket and touched the necklace. The cool metal kissed his sweaty flesh. That, at least, had been real.

There was something else, too, from before the fall. Something beyond the clearing. Something moving, darting through the bushes.

Rabbits! Henry thought, pushing himself to his knees and climbing out of the snow mound that had miraculously broken his fall and saved his life.

Henry started across the clearing, moving slowly at first, gingerly testing his legs to confirm they were okay. He felt a warm wetness on his face; he touched the cut above his eye. He dug into his pocket where his mother always stuffed a couple of tissues so he could blow his nose instead of sniffing, a bad habit he hadn't broken yet. He dabbed at the wound as he approached the edge of the clearing.

Henry pushed through the bushes and stepped onto a narrow path near where he had seen the hundreds of rabbits. The sight had been surreal and beautiful. There was no sign of them now, but their tracks remained in the freshly fallen snow.

Ahead of Henry was uncharted territory. He had never traveled in this direction before and he had no idea what might be waiting for him.

Henry studied the path, a snowy opening between the bushes and the trees. He remembered the warnings about the dangers of the forest and traveling alone. Bad things could happen to little boys who wandered off the marked trail. He had heard the stories.

But those rabbits....

Henry closed his eyes and saw them again. He wanted to discover where they had been headed in such an organized group. And why?

Yes, the forest could be dangerous, but he *had* survived that amazing fall, right? What could be worse than that? How could there possibly be anything more dangerous than that?

Henry glanced back at the dilapidated tree house, then turned and followed the rabbit tracks deeper into the woods.

THE PRESENT

(7)

Into the Cellar Again

When Henry returns to the kitchen, the house is eerily void of the strange sounds he heard earlier. He doesn't go straight for the cellar door, though. He wants to get something to light the way…and maybe a weapon, too, in case one of the rats is rabid.

Henry removes the child safety lock on the cabinets under the kitchen sink. There are cleaners and rags and sponges, along with a heavy Mag-Lite. There are no real weapons in the house. He grabs the flashlight and relocks the cabinets—ever mindful of the need to keep the cleaners and poisons locked away from Dillon's curious hands—and then he makes his way to the cellar door.

Henry pushes the door open, peeks around the corner into the darkness. He hears nothing. He sees nothing but the dark. The glow of the flashlight he dropped earlier is gone.

He points his Mag-Lite to cut through the gloom, illuminating a small patch of the dirt floor. He moves slowly down to the cellar, one step at a time, carefully listening and watching.

When Henry reaches the third step from the bottom, he quickly crouches and uses the Mag-Lite to search the cellar. The boiler is dark, silent. The other flashlight has been pushed into the far corner. The lens and bulb are shattered and coated with blood.

The blood is not human.

Surrounding the broken flashlight, littering the base of the boiler, are hundreds of dead rats, their bodies ripped to pieces, their intestines hanging from the boiler's pipes like jagged lengths of string, their beady eyes popped and leaking. The stench hits Henry like a fist and his stomach flips, sending bile into his mouth. He vomits onto the dirt floor, but he doesn't retreat, not yet. There is something even more disturbing and he can't take his eyes off it.

There is a freshly dug hole in the middle of the dirt floor. A big one. About the size of a grave. A mound of soil is piled off to the sides. Henry proceeds down the last two steps and carefully circles the hole, peering into it, afraid of what he will see. There's nothing. There's also no easy way to explain how the opening in the dirt came to be in such a short time.

Henry's whispers: "What the hell is going on?"

As if in reply, there's a harsh growl behind him from the direction of the boiler.

Henry spins at the sound, but the Mag-Lite is knocked from his hand before he can glimpse anything in the dark. The flashlight shatters against the stone wall, plunging the cellar into pitch darkness.

There's another growl, huge and echoing, and then something cold and sharp grabs at Henry's arms.

He screams and breaks free from the icy grip and spins around to flee and then, at the last second, he remembers the grave-like hole lurking between him and the stairs.

In his panic, he almost jumps directly into the low-lying support beams—but he realizes his error just in time and he dives forward like a kid playing Superman.

His momentum carries him across the grave and he lands hard and rolls onto the pile of freshly dug dirt.

He stumbles to his feet and he doesn't stop running until he has scaled the steps and he's in the attic again, locking the door and crawling into a darkened corner, pulling his legs up to his chest.

Henry can't believe what's happening; he's an adult and he must face reality head-on, but tears are pouring from his eyes. He can't remember ever being more scared than he is in this moment. He sniffles, reaches for his pocket for a tissue that isn't there.

Downstairs, there's a loud crash on the first floor. Then there's another crash. The fierce sounds grow louder and louder, closer and closer.

Henry hopes the attic door will protect him. If the door isn't enough, he doesn't think hiding in the darkness will be sufficient, either. But for now, he hides.

THE BIRTH OF THE ARTIST
(*8*)

When the tracks from the rabbits crossed the snow-covered open area located between the two sides of the forest, Henry knew he should stop and turn back. He could hear the roar of the water under the long and narrow clearing. This was the river, hidden under a blanket of ice and snow.

There was no path, but the rabbit tracks continued downstream, down the middle of the frozen river as if the death didn't lurk feet or inches below their paws. Henry followed their lead, but he didn't dare cross the river. Instead he did his best to stay on the snowy bank, but eventually the ground got steeper and steeper and he had to make a choice: go back into the woods or walk on the ice.

Henry couldn't stop thinking about the rabbits. Were they like the skeleton, just something he had dreamed up and simply imagined was real? How could he have imagined something so amazing, something he had never thought of or seen before? Baseball, football, cops and robbers, army men were all things he had watched on television. Even skeletons were a staple of his cartoons.

The rabbits with the red eyes were different. They *had* to be real if he had never seen them before. More importantly, he closed his eyes and reopened them a dozen times and the tracks never disappeared.

Henry carefully inched down the snowy back and onto the frozen river, a few small steps at a time. When his feet didn't break through, he trusted the ice to hold his weight more and more. Soon he was walking down the middle of the river, following the rabbit tracks as if this was just another path in the woods, one that roared liked a thunderstorm under his boots at times. He kept trying to imagine where the rabbits could have come from, and how they moved in sync like that, and why their eyes were red. And, most importantly, where were they going?

Henry was so lost in his thoughts he didn't hear the faint warning cries beneath him, the sound like glass being shattered in slow motion.

His first indication of the danger was when his right boot pushed through the ice and was grabbed by the frigid water, as if a hand had emerged from below to pull him down.

A shrill cry escaped Henry's throat. He took a step backwards and then he was sinking and an instant later the world was cold and black and he was struggling under the surface of the river, surrounded by a rushing wall of freezing water.

The current sucked Henry away from the hole he had created in the ice and into the darkness beyond. His eyes were wide and his arms flailed; the coldness slithered along his skin, chilling the blood in his veins, squeezing his chest.

Henry kicked his legs and he desperately held his breath as the swift current dragged him along. Vise-like pressure squeezed him from all sides and he couldn't believe what was happening. He felt trapped in a terrible nightmare.

His heart raced, yet his body was already becoming lethargic and sleepy from the biting cold.

Then, when Henry's eyes were about to close, when he was on the verge of letting the river carry him away, he smashed into the trunk of a submerged tree.

The pain was tremendous, but even though the water tugged at him with icy claws, the current wasn't dragging him along anymore and the shock jolted him back awake.

Henry wrapped his arms around the mossy trunk and pulled himself into the slick branches. His lungs were burning and screaming at him.

He looked up in desperation and saw the ice was only inches above him; he extended his arm weakly. His knuckles tapped at the frozen ceiling like he was pushing on solid rock.

He punched again with more force and a crack formed, the lines splintering away from him.

His third punch smashed the ice apart, opening a window into the cool winter sunlight.

Henry pulled himself up the branches and out of the water, sucking in a huge breath the moment he felt the dazzling embrace of the sun. He crawled up the tree toward the uprooted base of the trunk where the roots hung limply, exposed to the elements.

Once over land, Henry dropped to the snowy riverbank, gasping for air and staring into the sky at those dancing clouds. A chill was eating into his bones and he couldn't stop shivering. His teeth chattered and he bit down on one of his knuckles to make them stop.

Henry lay there in the snow, grateful to see the sky. He watched the clouds through a break in the trees. Exhaustion overwhelmed him. He couldn't imagine moving again, let alone crossing the river and finding his way home. He wanted to close his eyes and settle into the comfort of the cold darkness.

As the chill lulled Henry toward the grip of an endless sleep, a rustle came from the bushes.

The herd of white rabbits, hundreds of them, burst through the brush and stopped just short of where Henry lay.

Their noses and whiskers twitched and they stared at the little boy with their red eyes. *Follow us, there's more to see and do,* they seemed to say. Then they turned in unison and darted deeper into the forest.

Henry watched them go.

THE PRESENT

(8)

The Madness in the Cellar

*I*t *might be madness to believe there's a monster in* your cellar, but Henry is pretty sure denying what just happened to him would be an even worse kind of madness. The kind that ends with someone living in a padded room.

Henry is also beginning to believe he didn't need to discover an eye in the cellar drain to understand something was wrong in his home.

Under the surface, he has been sensing an intrusion into his peaceful world for longer than he cares to admit. Maybe even since he and Sarah bought the house. Maybe even *before* they bought the house. After all, the first time he felt worried here was when the real estate agent reluctantly showed him the steam boiler.

There's definitely something wrong and Henry doesn't have the slightest idea how he's supposed to fix it. He's an adult and adults fix problems, that much he knows. There aren't bogeymen in the real world, but he also knows what he felt and what he saw in the cellar. All of it was real.

There's another greasy thump from the second floor. Then another.

Henry looks out the window at the storm. The snow banks across the property are large and drifting; his little Honda in the garage is definitely no match for them. He watches the snow and the ice blowing in the wind and he wonders how far he could make it if he had to run for help.

Probably not very far. He doesn't even have his shoes on and there's no way he can get to them— they're in the bedroom on the second floor, well beyond whatever is stalking through the house.

As if to remind him he is trapped, the meaty *thump, thump* arrives at the bottom of the stairs to the attic. Whether or not that's a *real* monster doesn't really matter now. Something is down there and it's coming for Henry and if Henry's best defense is to hide in the dark, the results are going to be very unpleasant for him.

He only has one choice: the window.

He passes the unfinished painting he had been working on earlier when he left to care for the boiler, then stops suddenly in his tracks. There are splashes of red and gray and black across the canvas. The ancient dungeon has rough stone walls damp with blood and there are dead rats scattered across the brown dirt floor. Hidden in the darkness are red glowing eyes, hundreds of them. But the focus is the princess in her tattered gown. She stands between a lumbering monster and a small child, and she has raised the sword, as if preparing to charge the hideous beast.

Henry reaches for the canvas from yesterday, which he had faced at the wall with all of his other recent works so he couldn't see what he had painted.

The image is basically the same, but there is more distance between the princess and the monster. Henry moves down the line, turning the other paintings, none of which he can remember creating—just like he can't recall what he was thinking when he painted them.

They're all part of this series, which he's apparently been working on for at least a month. They're essentially the same image, with one small difference: the older the painting, the further the monster is from the princess. Very little changes otherwise. Just the depth of the shadows here or there, along with the number of the dead rats. Red eyes always glow in the darkness, watching the scene unfold.

What does this mean? Henry wonders.

There's another *thump, thump,* this time right outside the attic door.

Henry drops the painting and shoves the small attic window open, eliciting a cry from the monster behind the door. The winter wind smacks Henry in the face like a fist.

Snow blows into the attic as Henry climbs onto the slate roof, his hands already cold from gripping the splintering window frame. Once he's on the slick slate shingles, he closes the window again as the wind and snow whips past him. He watches through the window as the attic door bursts open and something slithers into the darkness.

Henry doesn't want to see what has come through the door. Instead he turns and crawls along the roof, the blistering wind biting into him. He's still only wearing his t-shirt and shorts, and the ice and snow against his legs and feet is so cold it burns him until his skin is numb.

He turns the corner at the side of the house, looks at the swaying tree in the front yard, then at the garage. That's where he has to go if he's to have any chance in this weather, but there's only one way to his destination: the fragile rose trellis that extends from the ground to the roof on the east side of the house, outside the kitchen window.

Henry begins to climb up toward the peak of the roof, taking the most direct route to the trellis. His hands ache from the chill; his entire body shakes.

He's crossing the peak when his right hand slips and he falls forward, landing chin first and sliding.

As his arms flail for anything he might be able to grab onto, two images flash in Henry's mind for the first time in years:

First is a crumbling tree house high above his head, a path of broken branches showing where gravity pulled him to the ground.

The second is a wall of ice holding him under a raging river as an icy rush of water attempted to suck the life out of him.

Henry has no time to analyze these images as he slides down the roof, plowing through the ice and the snow toward his cold and painful death.

The darkness envelopes him and he has almost accepted the inevitability of the fall when he slams into the stone chimney that directs the toxic fumes of the boiler away from the house and into the sky. He hadn't even seen the chimney in the snowy darkness, but he's never been more grateful for the awful old boiler in the cellar than he is at this moment.

Henry gasps, his arms wrapped around the chimney, his eyes staring past the gutter, down at the snowy lawn three stories below. The images of the tree house and the icy river are already fading from his mind.

With no time to catch his breath, Henry crawls the rest of the way to the top of the trellis. He swings his leg over the side and plants his bare foot as if this were a regular ladder.

The thorns dig into him like teeth; he bites his lip to keep from screaming. He swings his other leg over the edge. He has no choice but to ignore the pain while trusting the collection of interlaced wooden slats with his life. Where else can he go?

There's a slight groan as a few of the nails holding the trellis to the house pull free, and he's certain he'll fall this time, but Henry keeps moving slowly, lowering himself one careful step at a time, gritting his teeth as the rose thorns slice through his palms and his fingers, stab at his exposed arms and legs, and tear into his feet.

The pain in his hands and feet is nearly unbearable and when he finally arrives at the ground, he's bleeding from a dozen places, but he's alive.

THE BIRTH OF THE ARTIST
(9)

Henry knew he was too far from home, and he also knew he had to get out of his wet clothes and into a warm house sooner than later, so he did the only thing he could think to do: he followed the rabbit tracks. He pushed through the bushes and underbrush, stumbled down a hill and climbed another, all while trying to ignore the pain radiating from where his cold body had slammed into the tree.

Henry didn't understand what was happening, but he was experiencing more and more signs of delirium and exhaustion the further he went into the woods. Out of the corner of his eyes, he started to see movement. Little things at first, which he could explain away. That one shaking tree branch was due to a clump of snow falling from higher in the tree. Happens all the time after a snowstorm. Those two shaking branches? A couple of squirrels chasing each other, that's all.

But then, when entire trees were shaking and creaking with growls emerging from deep in their trunks—then Henry grew certain the forest was coming alive around him, stalking him.

Suddenly, Henry sensed one of the trees actually following him, having broken free of the ground, hulking after him and trying to grab onto his yellow raincoat. There were thunderous footsteps chasing after him and the entire world shook from the impacts.

Henry jumped in surprise, started to run... but then he looked over his shoulder in terror and realized the tree hadn't moved, of course. Maybe none of them had. He stopped running, his chest heaving, his body exhausted.

Henry continued following the rabbit tracks, much more slowly, but soon he heard strange sounds like thousands of birds gathering in the trees above him. They were flapping their wings incessantly and cawing shrilly. He could feel their beady eyes tracking him as he in turn tracked the rabbits, which were following deer trails deeper into the darkest, thickest part of the woods.

Eventually the tracks started up another hill, but Henry slowed to a stop in the snowy brush at the bottom. He wasn't sure he had the strength to go on. The woods were as dark as night, and the cawing of the birds was louder than ever, and he couldn't shake the idea that something was following him, even though he saw nothing when he spun around and looked where he had just come from. There was movement everywhere, but it was always just out of his field of vision.

I need to find out what's at the top of this hill, he thought, tracing the tracks with his eyes. *Maybe the rabbits will be waiting for me.*

Or maybe not. At least he would know. He promised himself he would at least check the top of this hill. If he didn't find the rabbits, he would start running home until he couldn't run anymore, leaving the evil woods far behind.

Henry climbed the hill, his legs burning from the strain. The birds screamed at him, the trees rustled and started pulling out of the ground again to follow him. Dark and light danced around him. His heart raced in terror, and he fell to his knees and crawled, pulling himself along with his hands.

He got to his feet again, but he stumbled at the top of the hill, landing on his side in a beam of sunlight breaking through the tree cover.

Henry's eyes wanted to close, he didn't want to see whatever monsters were about to devour him, but he made himself look around like he had promised himself—and when he saw where he was, his eyes widened and he felt his heart leap in his chest.

The river route had taken him the entire way around town. Beyond the underbrush was a plowed parking lot and beyond the icy pavement was the Black Hill Community School. His father's station wagon was parked by the front doors. There were no other cars in sight.

Henry got to his feet, his mind suddenly very clear. The birds had vanished,the trees were back to normal and the daylight was bright and safe.

With newfound strength, Henry climbed the snow bank created by the plow earlier in the day and he crossed the parking lot, taking care to avoid the slick spots. Mountains of plowed snow surrounded the tall light poles.

Henry stopped on the far side of the parking lot. The rabbit tracks appeared there again, leading directly to the school's front doors, only this time the tracks weren't soft indentations in the snow.

They were made out of blood.

Henry carefully approached the front doors, confused by the tracks and trying to decide how to explain to his father what he was doing here and why he was soaked to the bone. His mother would ground him for life if she learned where he had gone, and Ms. Winslow would probably never let him leave the house again, but the cold was crushing him and he had to get into the warmth.

When Henry pulled on the door, he was surprised it opened so easily. He had assumed the doors would be locked since the school was closed for the day.

He stepped into the well-lit hallway where the trail of bloody rabbit tracks continued, covering the floor between the rows of lockers.

The school was as silent as a tomb, with the exception of the buzzing lights above his head. There was no one to be seen anywhere.

Then the door slammed shut behind Henry and he was left standing alone in the hallway. Only he wasn't alone. The coldness in his bones told him so.

THE PRESENT

(9)

Preparing to Battle the Beast

Henry *is standing in the snow at the bottom of* the rose trellis, wrapping his bleeding hands and feet with pieces of his shredded t-shirt when he hears the phone ringing in the kitchen. The sound is far away, but he recognizes the shrill noise in the gusting winter wind. He and Sarah have wanted to replace the antique phone since the first time it rang in their presence, the harsh buzzing scaring them both. Like a lot of things, they just hadn't gotten around to it yet.

Henry peers through the kitchen window. There's no monster to be seen, but the table is smashed and the phone is on the floor, nearly ripped from the wall. Cabinets are open, pots and pans are strewn about, and plates and glasses are broken into jagged shards.

Henry wants to ignore the phone, but there's only one person who might be calling and he needs to speak with her if he's going to die today, a possibility he's coming to accept now that he's bleeding and shivering and the cold is moving up his spine into his brain.

He hurries to the back door, which is locked, and he smashes a panel of frost-coated glass with his elbow. The pain is faster and sharper than he expected. He reaches through the broken glass and unlocks the deadbolt, pushes the door open with a shove.

He carefully crosses the kitchen, watching for any sign of whatever made this mess. The house is quiet, with the exception of the phone. He tries to avoid the broken glass and shards of china— the remains of a wedding gift from his in-laws— on the linoleum and he grimaces in pain as each unavoidable piece becomes lodged into his foot.

Henry lifts the receiver and answers with a quick: "Hello? Hello?"

"Henry?" the crackling voice on the line replies. "Henry, I can barely hear you!"

"Sarah?"

"Henry, if you can hear me, we're at the end of the driveway. You didn't answer the phone, I've been calling since last night, so I tried to make it home…"

The line goes to static, then clears.

"…we're stuck and the battery died about an hour ago. We're going to try for the house…"

The line goes to static.

"…build a nice warm fire, okay? Henry? Can you hear me, Henry? I love you, okay? I want you to…."

And then the line dies.

"Sarah, no!" Henry yells. He slams the phone and tries to dial, but there's no dial tone.

Henry fully understands what he heard: his wife and his little boy are a mile away, trapped out in the storm, and they're going to try to travel on foot to the house. That's insane! It's freezing, but is it too cold to spend the night in the van? Henry doesn't know, but Sarah must think so or she wouldn't endanger Dillon.

Henry has to help his wife and son, he has to find a way…but then he hears another wet thump from the cellar…and then there's a deep, bitter laugh, too, as if the monster senses more food is coming.

Henry understands this truth in his gut. He drops the phone and runs back into the snowy night, focused on his original destination: the garage. Now he has a different reason for going there. If he can accept that monsters are real, all he has to do is ask himself one question: how do you destroy a monster? The answer is simple and he feels almost giddy. The answer is obvious now that he's thought of it.

Again the ice and snow is soothing on Henry's battered and bruised and bloody feet. The chill crawling through his bones is numbing him to the pain, but he isn't sure that's a good thing. Once he arrives at the garage door, Henry breaks yet another window. His keys are on the hook by the kitchen door, but he never thought of them and he has no time to waste.

Inside the garage, the walls offer him shelter from the weather, although the air is brisk. His little Honda sits by the garage door, alone in the middle of the empty space. There's no clutter here, unlike the cellar. In the far corner is the riding lawnmower and the rakes and the red gas can. There are also old cans of house paint and rough paintbrushes and a bag full of torn rags.

Henry grabs the cleanest rag he can find and he gently brushes the glass and broken china off his feet. Next he removes the rose thorns hidden under the blood on his flesh, but some are pushed so deep it'll take tweezers to get them. He doesn't have that kind of time.

Henry wraps his feet with the paint rags and he hobbles to his riding lawnmower. There, in the corner, are his work boots, which he had kicked off here the previous fall so he wouldn't track mud into the house. He slips the boots on and ties the laces tight, grunting as the thorns he missed are pushed deeper into his foot.

Next Henry grabs a deck mop from the rack next to the lawn mower. He snaps open the lid on the red container of gasoline and pours the liquid over the mop's strands of thick yarn.

And then Henry is back out the door and into the storm.

THE BIRTH OF THE ARTIST
(10)

The bloody rabbit tracks covered the school's lime colored linoleum floor, from one wall to the other. Henry took a few tentative steps further into the hallway where the eerie emptiness greeted him with each step. The sound of his boots echoed between the metal lockers. The rows of lights high above his head hummed.

Henry was shivering, but he had forgotten the cold; curiosity pushed him to follow the tracks. He moved slowly at first, still expecting to be caught by a teacher or maybe even the principal, but he increased his pace when it became clear he was alone. The classrooms were empty and those dozens and dozens of empty desks, along with the previous day's lessons on the chalkboards, were vaguely unsettling, as if everyone had vanished in the middle of class and would never return.

The rabbit tracks led Henry past the dark cafeteria and into the band hallway until they disappeared again at a closed metal door marked MAINTENANCE ONLY. Henry knew this door. His father had brought him here once. This door was how you got to the basement and all of the boilers with their girl names: Hillary, Matilda, Gertrude, Amelia. This was where his father drained the fat bears.

Henry pushed on the door and it swung open. The tracks continued down the concrete steps, but the space was narrow and the tracks smudged together into a river of blood, dripping from step to step. Henry stood at the top of the stairs, gazing into the dim room below. Then came the sound:

Thump-thump-thump.

Henry heard this call of the boilers, crisp and clear at first—but then the noise was miles away and his vision was spinning. The stairs twisted and turned, the dim light bulbs flickered and flashed, and he heard the crackle of running water off in the distance.

Thump-thump-thump.

Henry stood at the top of the stairs, one hand clutching the slim metal railing, the other hand cold against the wall, and he closed his eyes. The tremendous darkness behind his eyelids began to rotate and he could see colors, the same kind of colors that sometimes came to him when he was playing games in the backyard. Bright white stars burst to life. His fingers tightened on the railing, but he didn't step backwards, he didn't sit. He couldn't do anything but stand there.

Four words appeared in the darkness, followed by his name, which glowed bright red within the star-spotted void. The stars spun clockwise and the words twisted and rotated and changed places until they settled into their final positions.

The words were: *Henry paints* against *the darkness.*

When Henry opened his eyes, the stairs had returned to normal. The walls were no longer damp and the light in the room below was steady. Yet the sound of the running water hadn't gone away. In fact, it was louder, somehow clearer, although he couldn't see it.

There was another change, too. The bloody rabbit tracks had vanished. Henry looked around, confused, but there was no sign the rabbits had ever been in the school.

The sound of the water grew louder, and Henry made his way to the bottom of the steps. This was the break room for the maintenance employees. There were seven metal lockers, two wooden benches, a duct-taped couch, a yellowed refrigerator, and an old television tuned to a golf tournament. There were no windows and the floor looked grimy in the buzzing light.

On the far side of the room was a door labeled DANGER: BOILERS. That was where Henry's father drained the fat bears.

Henry approached the door. The sound of the running water was even louder now.

"Stupid fat bear, c'mon, you bitch!" his father cried from behind the door.

Henry stopped. He had never heard his father speak like this, with this much anger. Henry pulled the door open a crack and he was even more shocked by what he saw.

One of the boilers had sprung a leak. Water was spraying like a fire hose against the concrete walls, which were old and dark like a dungeon.

Henry's father was fighting with the emergency shutoff value, twisting a gigantic wrench with all his might. His arms were bulging and a vein was popping out of his forehead. His overalls and work boots were soaked in the dirty water, which was slowly filling the room. The large drain in the middle of the floor couldn't maintain the pace. The water churned around his father, who was fighting desperately to stop the flow.

Then Henry saw the monsters for the first time, lurking in the shadows. They rose from the water, their scaly hunchbacks ascending like a shark's fin. Their scarred faces came next, followed by twisted arms and curled hands with razor-sharp claws. The monsters scowled at Henry as they edged closer to his father...but he couldn't believe they were real. This had to be another one of his imaginary worlds, another one of his games, just like he plays in the backyard or like the skeleton in the tree house and the rabbits with the red eyes—but his imaginary games never terrified him like this.

"Daddy?" Henry said, nervously.

His father looked up in surprise at the sound of his son's voice and in that moment one of the monsters grabbed the giant wrench, twisting it with an inhuman force, snapping the emergency shutoff value in half.

The boiler hissed and released its pent-up pressure directly onto Henry's father, shredding his shirt and instantly scalding him like he had been dropped into a fryer. His skin peeled off in layers, bloody and horrible. He dropped to his knees, his face melting.

"Daddy!" Henry screamed.

The stream of boiling hot water slowed to a trickle and the ear-piercing hiss ended. There was a deathly silence unlike any Henry had ever experienced in his life. Then the monsters pounced on his father, digging into his exposed flesh with their fangs, sending a wave of blood across the room. The chewing sound was horrible—and within seconds the cooked flesh was ripped from his father's bones.

As the monsters fed, Henry's father fell forward into the water, a pool of blood spreading from his body.

Henry gazed at the red eyes of the monsters as they devoured the thick strands of meat—and then he ran from the basement screaming and he didn't stop running or screaming until he found his way home where he would hide under his bed until the darkness came.

THE PRESENT

(10)

Against the Darkness

Henry pushes the door open, and again there is no sign of whatever has trashed the house. He steps into the kitchen. This time the broken glass and china crunch under his work boots. He stops at the sink and opens the cabinets one more time, retrieving the matches Sarah purchased to light their Christmas candles.

When Henry arrives at the bottom of the cellar stairs, he lights one of the matches and tosses it at the end of the mop. The strands of cloth explode into flames. The sight is impressive.

Henry uses the flaming mop to cut a fiery path through the darkness. The monster— whatever it might be—may not have been afraid to knock the flashlight out of his hands, but Henry is betting fire will be a different story. Fire has always defeated monsters in fairy tales.

There are now three graves in the dirt floor, two large, one small. Beyond them is the boiler and the mutilated remains of the rats...but the boiler no longer appears to be made entirely of metal and asbestos. Although the middle is still firmly attached to the floor, the twisting pipes have transformed into scaly arms—dozens of them, reaching and twisting and pulling. The boiler's metal door on the fat belly grins at Henry, showing a frightening hint of the raging fire inside.

The monster says: "Hello, Henry."

Henry gasps as the memories come pouring back: the woods that snowy day when he was five, the tree house, the river, his father's apparent death, and most importantly, his father's return that evening, alive and well with not a mark on him. Henry had locked these memories into the furthest corner of his mind, behind a wall of stone he didn't realize was there.

In this moment, as Henry faces another monster, he understands those events were all true—not necessarily *real,* but true. Everything may not have happened exactly the way he thought it was happening—his imagination was a wild place—but there was an underlying truth to what he saw. Which means…

"None of this is real," Henry whispers.

"Silly little boy. You accepted me as real when you were still wetting the bed. You can't back out now."

Henry considers this and says: "I don't *want* this to be real."

"Henry, I didn't call myself into this world. That beautifully twisted mind of yours did. You called me, you keep me. That's the way life works."

"Then go away. I'll make you go away."

One of the monster's scaly arms rises and points at the flaming mop, which looks much less impressive in the light of the boiler's flaming belly. The monster says: "You think a little fire will stop me from eating your family? I'm a fat bear with my own fire in my belly, you silly little boy."

The boiler shivers as the asbestos continues the transformation into sharp scales. The top of the boiler bulges into a meaty hunchback, the flesh writhing and twitching. The metal door grins at Henry, showing off newly-grown fangs.

Henry realizes the mistake he has made. Fire isn't going to do anything to stop this creature. It loves fire and heat. It lives for the fire.

Henry takes a step backwards, throws the flaming mop in desperation, and then he sprints up the stairs again. The boiler swallows the mop in one big gulp.

"You can run from me, Henry," the monster calls, "but I'll always find you. I'll always be with you, no matter how far or how fast you run! You called *me*, remember?"

Henry hears this but he doesn't really hear it. He's bounding up the steps two at a time and through the first floor, not even seeing the smashed furniture and broken plaster and all the damage the boiler inflicted upon the house with those dreadful arms.

Once in the attic, Henry slams the door and falls to his knees. His heart is pounding and tears are dotting his face. He holds his head with his hands, pulling at his hair, and he studies what remains of his studio.

Paintings are shredded—including the Princess in the Dungeon series he never liked anyway—and paint is spilled everywhere. There are splashes of red on the walls, white on the ceiling, blue on the floor, green on the window.

A single blank canvas remains untouched in the middle of the room.

Just start at the beginning, Henry's father whispers in his mind, *and the rest will take care of itself.*

"The beginning? What does that mean?"

Just start at the beginning.

"This afternoon when I couldn't paint?"

Further back.

Henry closes his eyes. "The Princess in the Dungeon?"

Further.

Henry pulls his hair. The pain is sharp and his mind flashes on an image of a tree house and the coldness of the snow and the ice on the river and....

"The day when I was five?"

Yes! is the thunderous reply.

And finally Henry understands. The answer was there in his father's advice all along. He grabs a blank canvas and his paint palette and he shoves a brush into his pocket. He runs downstairs toward the cellar, again taking the steps two at a time, almost tripping on his own feet in his hurry.

He doesn't slow, he doesn't let himself think. Thinking gets in the way; thinking will create doubts, build walls. He had the right idea the first time—he just took the wrong weapon with him.

I paint against *the darkness,* Henry thinks as he navigates his way through the trashed first floor to the kitchen and the cellar steps.

He slips on the broken glass in the kitchen, slams into the wall next to the cellar door. His leg twists awkwardly, but he stays on his feet. He hobbles down the narrow wooden steps and then he trips and falls onto the dirt cellar floor. The canvas flies from his hands.

The cellar is dark and damp, except for the light from the fire in the boiler's belly whenever the monster speaks.

"Decided to give yourself to me?" the boiler asks, showing its new metal fangs again.

Henry ignores the question, getting to his feet. He retrieves the canvas and leans it against the mound of dirt next to the three graves. He pulls the paintbrush from his pocket and jabs it through the paint on his palette without even looking.

"What are you doing?" the monster demands.

I paint against *the darkness,* Henry thinks, but he doesn't answer. He closes his eyes and applies the paint to the canvas just like when he works in the dark in the middle of the night. He doesn't need to see what he's doing. The image in his mind is larger than life.

The Princess appears, holding her sword, putting herself between the monster and the little boy in the dungeon. Henry sees for the first time that *he* is the child.

The monster, lurking in the corner of the scene, is hunched over, drool dripping from sharp fangs. The monster growls and breathes fire at the Princess. Her flowing gown, which is already tattered and torn, bursts into flames, but she protects the little boy with her body.

Then, releasing a fierce battle cry, she charges at the monster, a trail of flames flowing behind her like beads of water in the air.

The Princess slices at the monster with her sword; he deflects her blow with his massive arms. The sound is odd, though, like steel on steel instead of flesh.

The boiler screams, but Henry barely hears. He continues to paint, his brush moving from the palette to the canvas so quickly his arm is a blur. Paint splashes on his clothes, the dirt floor, the wooden beams, the stone walls.

Thump-thump-thump, cries the boiler.

In Henry's mind, streaks of colors circle the Princess, swirling and dancing like the fiery bubbles trailing her wherever she goes. She grunts and swings her sword and this time one of the monster's arms goes flying in a splash of blood.

The boiler screams.

Henry feels an electrical current in the air. There's heat pounding him like the hottest summer day.

In Henry's mind, the monster fights back, grabbing the Princess and throwing her across the dungeon, nearly knocking the little boy down. The boy stands frozen in shock, unable to help or run.

In the cellar, one of the boiler's pipes strikes Henry in the chest. He falls backwards, the breath ripped from his lungs, but he jumps right back to the canvas without opening his eyes and he continues his work without missing a beat.

Thump-thump-thump.

Using a mix of white and gray, Henry adds a wavy bubble of hard air around the Princess and the little boy on the canvas.

The Princess charges again. The monster takes a swing at her, but the razor sharp claws simply break off when they connect with the protective bubble.

The monster screams and so does the boiler.

The colors swirl faster around the Princess, brighter and more vivid.

The monster backs away from her, into a corner.

Thump-thump-thump, cries the boiler.

The Princess—still on fire and badly injured—shows her teeth through a fierce grin as she charges one last time, driving the sword into the moist belly of the beast.

The monster and the boiler scream—and a second later, Henry is engulfed by the roar of an explosion; a wave of heat blows past him and up the cellar stairs.

He opens his eyes. The boiler is shredded and the entire cellar is burning. The brightness of the fire hurts his eyes and the heat makes his skin throb. Yet the flames do not touch him; they're held at bay by an invisible bubble surrounding Henry. The sight is like taking a peek through a portal into Hell.

Henry feels a surge of triumph, but it is short-lived. The monster is dead, but the explosion damaged the line from the oil tank to the boiler. Black liquid is squirting on the stone walls.

Henry's eyes widen and he clutches his paintbrush tightly as he sprints up the stairs to the kitchen one last time. He continues out the door and he's halfway to the garage when the house explodes in a flash of intense white light, knocking him off his feet. The noise is deafening and the entire world glows brightly like a star supernova and then quickly fades to black.

THE BIRTH OF THE ARTIST
(11)

Henry was sniffling and hiding under his bed when he heard the front door of the house open and close. The room had grown dark as the sun disappeared for the day and he was still wearing his yellow rain slicker. His clothing was soaked in sweat, his face was wet with tears. A puddle from the snow melting off his boots trickled across the hardwood floor. He sobbed until his eyes burned.

The bedroom door opened and his father's familiar work boots crossed the room, landing every step with a dull thud.

His father's pants were stained with grease and grime and bleach. He took a knee and then, after a brief moment, his weathered, callused hand reached under the bed. Henry grabbed onto the hand, not believing it was really there, but his father gently pulled him out from under the bed just the same.

"What are you doing under there?" his father asked.

"The monsters…I saw the monsters get you," Henry whimpered before sobbing uncontrollably again.

"Son, that's silly. What do you mean?"

Henry couldn't stop crying, couldn't even get the words to form.

His father said: "It'll be okay, Henry. Just start at the beginning and the rest will take care of itself."

While Henry's father helped him out of his rain slicker and into some dry clothing, Henry told him everything he had seen and done, including the fall from the tree house, the herd of rabbits, the trip down the river, and the monsters in the boiler room of the school.

Henry's father held him and rocked him while he cried some more. His father said: "Well, Henry, it sounds like your imagination really got away from you today, didn't it?"

Henry only nodded, unable to believe none of what happened had been real. He had the cuts on his face from the fall, after all, and his heart ached with a deep pain.

His father said, "When the weather gets a little nicer, we'll go look at that tree house together, what do you say?"

Henry nodded.

"You okay?"

Henry shook his head and blurted: "I was so scared of the monsters!"

"Henry," his father said, "the monsters don't live in the dark corners waiting to pounce on us. They live deep in our heart. But we can fight them. I promise you, we can fight them and we can win. Why don't you get a piece of paper and some crayons. I know something that'll help you feel better."

Henry retrieved his paper and his crayons and he sat on the floor in the beam of moonlight coming through the window.

"Okay, draw the clearing with the tree house," his father instructed, standing next to him.

Henry did as his father told him to the best of his ability, using his green and brown crayons.

"Now, add the skeleton you told me about."

Henry hesitated. He didn't want to think about the skeleton anymore.

"It's okay, trust me."

Henry didn't have a white crayon, so he used yellow. The skeleton was sort of hanging off the tree, drawn on top of the branches.

"Now, put a big red X over it."

Henry looked up at his father, who simply nodded at the paper.

Again, Henry did as his father instructed, only instead of drawing an X, he crossed back and forth over the skeleton a dozen times with the red crayon.

"Good! Use the yellow to add a nice happy sun."

Henry was already feeling better and he suddenly understood what his father was showing him: he could remove the bad and scary things from the pictures and replace them with something he liked better. Maybe he couldn't make those changes in the real world, but he certainly could in his imagination. And if removing those bad things and adding the good things on paper made him feel better *inside*, that was okay, right?

Henry's father handed him another sheet of paper and this time Henry drew the frozen river at the moment the ice began to crack. He didn't need his father's guidance now that he understood the power of what he was doing.

In fact, within minutes Henry didn't even feel like he was sitting in his bedroom. He wasn't seeing the paper and the crayons in the moonlight. Instead he was on the river again, hearing the ice cracking—and then fixing it. As he built this imaginary world around himself, he created a place where he didn't fall through the ice or out of the tree house, where there were no scary birds in the trees and no monsters in the basement of the school.

For the first time, Henry was able to cross between the imaginary worlds he created in the backyard and transfer them into the real world simply by drawing the images on the paper.

Eventually his father slipped away and Henry continued to draw deep into the night. And as Henry worked, the words he had seen in the colorful darkness behind his eyes appeared in his mind again.

I paint against *the darkness,* Henry thought.

He liked the sound of that. Those words made him feel strong in a way he couldn't describe. Those words opened doors within his mind; they set him free and they gave him the courage to face the darkest night. He was no longer afraid of the terrifying things he was drawing. After all, he could make them go away the moment they got too scary.

I paint against *the darkness.*

The monsters were simply shadows to be erased or drawn over, nothing more, nothing less.

THE PRESENT

(11)

A Family Found

Henry is numb, but gloved hands are shaking him. He rolls over in the snow and stares into the darkness and at first he sees nothing but a memory:

Gray and blue sky, clouds gliding to the east. A tree towering above him. A hole in the floor of a dilapidated tree house. A skeleton wearing a yellow rain slicker and boots. A chain necklace, a tarnished silver crucifix.

With his bruised and bloody hands, Henry touches inside his tattered shirt, feels the metal pressing on his chest. After all of these years, he still wears the necklace he found in the tree house when he was a boy. Even after he forgot where it came from, he has worn the necklace every day, touching it for comfort without knowing why.

Then the darkness rushes into Henry's field of vision before being pushed away by the dancing orange light engulfing him: the blazing inferno that was once his home.

Out of the darkness above comes the snow, falling in waves.

And then, finally, Sarah's face appears. And little Dillon. His cheeks are red and round, his eyes wide. Henry's wife and son are speaking, but he can't yet hear the words. They're both beautiful like angels.

Henry closes his eyes and his imagination shows him what will happen next:

He and his family huddling in the garage around a small fire, which they'll start with the burning debris spread across their snowy lawn.

His family watching the storm pound the countryside for the rest of the night while their home burns into the cellar.

The fire department and the police arriving in the morning after the storm, when someone reports the thick black smoke.

His family being driven from the property, never to return.

Their search for a new home where he'll build a new studio...but this time, Henry will stay in control of his imagination, he won't let the imaginary world trapped inside his mind control his real life. Not ever again.

And as the coldness wraps around Henry, he smiles and he hugs his wife and his son—and he vows to never let them go, no matter what.

THE BIRTH OF THE ARTIST
(*12*)

When Henry's mother came into his bedroom, it was long after midnight and Henry was drawing intensely in the dark. He was dressed in his pajamas and an unfamiliar silver crucifix dangled from his neck, nearly touching the floor as he crouched over his paper.

"Henry! Are you okay?" his mother cried, throwing herself to her knees and hugging her son tightly. He barely flinched, just continued with his work.

When his mother saw this, she grabbed his hand, breaking the crayon in his palm with a sharp snap. That shook Henry from his waking dream, from the place he had gone while he was drawing, his imaginary world.

"What's wrong?" Henry asked when he saw the smeared mascara on his mother's face and the fresh tears pouring from her eyes. He had never seen his mother like this in his entire life. She was always radiant and lovely in the way only a mother can be to her children.

"Henry, where have you been?" she asked, wiping her eyes.

Henry grew even more confused when the State Police officer stepped into the room and turned on the light. The light was blinding and somehow awful; Henry blinked and covered his face.

"Mommy, what's wrong?"

"Henry," his mother said, wiping her eyes with one hand while holding on to her son's arm with the other, as if to make sure he was truly real. "Ms. Winslow reported you missing this afternoon. We've been searching for you for hours!"

She started sobbing and pulled him tight. Henry was stunned. He said: "What do you mean? Dad knew where I was."

Henry's mother couldn't stop crying and she didn't respond.

"Mommy, what's wrong?"

"Son," the State Trooper said, kneeling and stroking Henry's hair, "I'm afraid I have some bad news. Your father died in an accident at the school today. I'm very sorry."

Henry shook his head. No, that wasn't right. He struggled to free himself from his mother's grip, but she wouldn't let go. Henry started to cry and shake—not because the State Trooper said his father was dead, but because his mother wouldn't loosen her grip, not even a little. Didn't she understand? Henry could fix this, but he had to get to his paper and his crayons. He could make the bad things disappear if she'd just let him!

"*I paint* against *the darkness*," Henry said as he fought to pull himself free from his mother.

But his mother kept holding Henry as tight as she could, as if she planned to never let him go again, and the State Trooper returned to the living room to give them some privacy while he called off the search for the missing boy.

ABOUT THE AUTHOR

Brian James Freeman is the author of many short stories, essays, non-fiction, novellas, and novels. He is also the publisher of Lonely Road Books where he has worked with Stephen King, Mick Garris, Stewart O'Nan, and other acclaimed authors. Brian lives in Pennsylvania with his wife, two cats, and two German Shorthaired Pointers who are afraid of the cats. More books are on the way. Visit him on the web at www.BrianJamesFreeman.com

2947415R00080

Printed in Great Britain
by Amazon.co.uk, Ltd.,
Marston Gate.